THE VERY HUNGRY BEAR

NICK BLAND

Scholastic Canada Ltd.

Toronto New York London Auckland Sydney
Mexico City New Delhi Hong Kong Buenos Aires

For Andrew McMillan

Scholastic Canada Ltd.
604 King Street West, Toronto, Ontario M5V 1E1, Canada

Scholastic Inc.
557 Broadway, New York, NY 10012, USA

Scholastic Australia Pty Limited
PO Box 579, Gosford, NSW 2250, Australia

Scholastic New Zealand Limited
Private Bag 94407, Botany, Manukau 2163, New Zealand

Scholastic Children's Books
Euston House, 24 Eversholt Street, London NW1 1DB, UK

Nick used acrylic paint on paper to create these illustrations.
Typeset in Geist Serifa.

Library and Archives Canada Cataloguing in Publication

Bland, Nick, 1973-
The very hungry bear / Nick Bland.

ISBN 978-1-4431-1906-1 (bound).--ISBN 978-1-4431-1907-8 (pbk.)

I. Title.

PZ10.3.B527Veh 2012   j823'.92   C2011-908423-6

First published by Scholastic Australia in 2012.
This edition published in Canada by Scholastic Canada Ltd. in 2012.

Text and illustrations copyright © Nick Bland, 2012.

7 6 5 4 3   Printed in Malaysia 108   15 16 17 18 19

Bear was in a **GRUMPY** mood,
he hadn't eaten any food,
and he couldn't catch a single fish to cook.

He'd been hungry since the break of day
and every fish had got away . . .

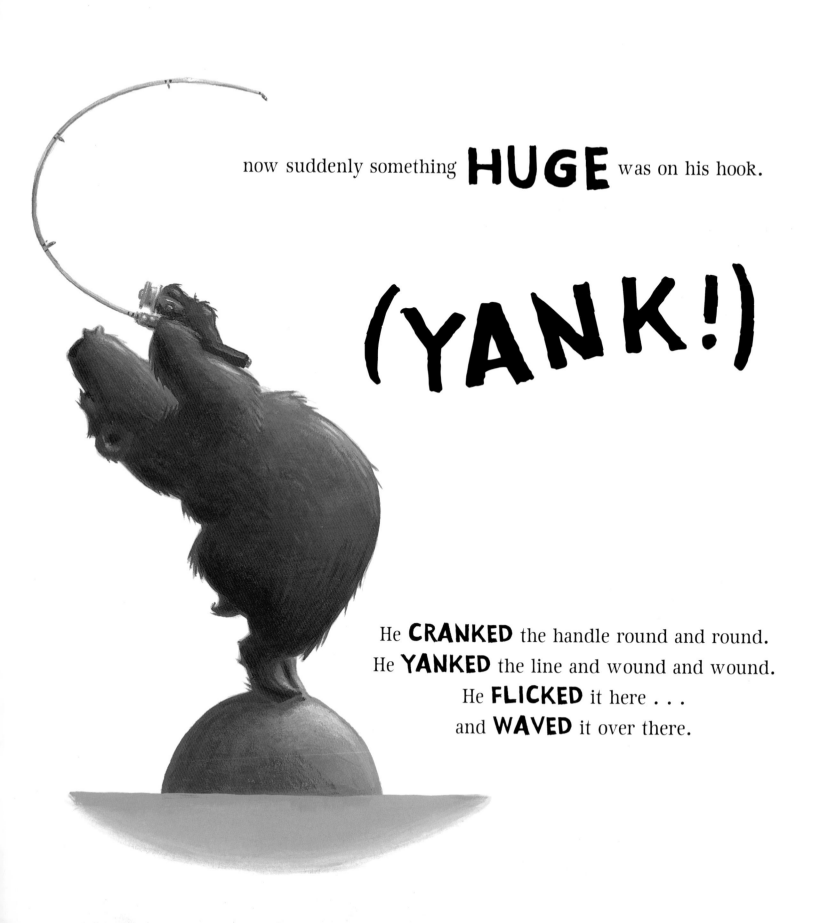

now suddenly something **HUGE** was on his hook.

(YANK!)

He **CRANKED** the handle round and round.
He **YANKED** the line and wound and wound.
He **FLICKED** it here . . .
and **WAVED** it over there.

A **HUNGRY** bear is very strong,
so it didn't take him very long
to discover that he'd caught . . .

A POLAR BEAR!

"Excuse me," said Bear.
"Do you have to fish there?
You are catching all of the fish."

"I'm sorry," he said,
as he lifted his head.
"You can have one of mine if you wish."

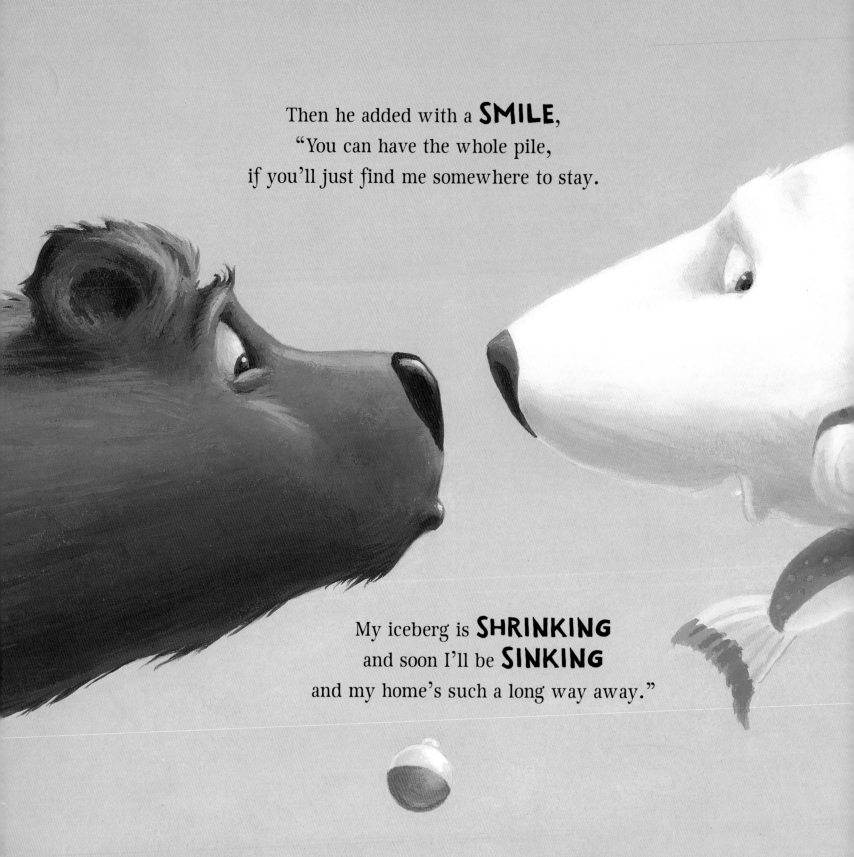

Then he added with a **SMILE**,
"You can have the whole pile,
if you'll just find me somewhere to stay.

My iceberg is **SHRINKING**
and soon I'll be **SINKING**
and my home's such a long way away."

Now a fish to a bear
is like a chocolate éclair —
it's **INCREDIBLY** hard to resist.

So the thought of a pile
that would last for a while
was an offer too good to be missed!

With a **SPLOSH** and a **SPLISH**
and an armful of fish,
Bear led the way through the trees.

"My cave's over there
and I'm happy to **SHARE**.
You can stay for as long as you please."

But his guest shook his head,
"I'm so sorry," he said.
"While your cave is particularly nice,

it's just a bit **HOT**
for this coat that I've got,
and the fire is **MELTING** my ice."

So they went to see Mole
and he dug them a hole,
which was cooler . . . but
just a bit small.

And they visited Croc,
on his cool river rock.
But he wasn't that helpful at all.

"Perhaps this is **BEST!**"
said the bear, from a nest.
"But I think that I'm going
to **SNEEZE!**"

Then he squinted his eyes
and he said with surprise,
"**AHHH...**

CHOO!

I'm **ALLERGIC** to trees."

So the bear with white hair
followed right behind Bear
to the only place left they could go.
Away from the trees
and the warm summer breeze . . .

all the way **UP** to the **SNOW**.

They built him a home
with an icy-white dome,

and Bear left a **HOUSE-WARMING** dish.

With a **SMILE** and a **WAVE**
Bear went back to his cave . . .

and he stopped on the way

FOR A FISH.